Wolf Lover:
KONOCHUR

New Scotia Pack, Book 2

Victoria Danann

ORDER OF THE
BLACK SWAN

If you're interested in serving on the best street team in the universe, email blackswanjunkie@gmail.com or visit here www.victoriadanann.com/the-street-team.

A TEAM MEMBERS WHO SERVED AS BETA READERS for
Wolf Lover: Konochur

PROLOGUE

✖

THE ORDER OF THE BLACK SWAN

This book is loosely related to the Knights of Black Swan series and contains a few minor references to characters from those books.

There is a very old and secret society of vampire hunters, paranormal investigators and protectors known as The Order of the Black Swan. In the twenty-first century, the Order was presented with proof that the scientific postulation that multiple dimensions operate independently within the same "space", tied to one planet as hub or anchor, depending on how you view it. Each dimension is a single reality to its occupants with the exception of Elementals – demons, angels, sylphs, and certain shifters, who can move between dimensions as easily as we walk from room to room.

THE NEW SCOTIA TRIBE

From *Moonlight*, Book 4, Knights of Black Swan. In the process of averting possible extinction of his tribe, the king of the Elk Mountain werewolves, Stalkson Grey, fell in love with a cult slave and abducted her with the demon, Deliverance's, assistance. He eventually won his captive's heart and took his new mate to the New Elk Mountain werewolf colony in Lunark Dimension where the wolf people's ancestors had settled centuries before. The Elk Mountain tribe had ceased to produce daughters for an entire generation. The demon found a solution to that by locating a human world that had not produced sons. The werewolf boys were given a month to find mates and convince them to leave their homes for an unknown place called Lunark.

A few years later his nephew-by-marriage, (*Liulf*, New Scotia Pack Book 1), also migrated his tribe to Lunark Dimension and set up the colony of New Scotia. This book is about his younger brother and second-in-command, Konochur, called Conn and the human, Lestriv, who had married one of the werewolves and pioneered migration to a new world.

CHAPTER 1

✖

"*THEY'RE HERE!*"

Lessie smiled at the excitement in Elise's voice. She turned her face toward where Elise was pointing while jumping up and down.

She laughed at her friend. "Have a little dignity."

"Pffft," said Elise. "Who needs dignity? I need a man. Or maybe a werewolf man." She pretended to swoon.

The day was bright, filled with the musical sounds of wind chimes ringing in the breeze, like a fanfare announcing the arrival of the young wolves looking for brides. Lessie tried but failed to calm the surge of nerves. Elise was the catalyst that pushed her control over the edge. Her emotions had broken free and were not taking either advice or direction, as was clear by the goose bumps that had risen all over her body.

Even the air felt like it was filled with magic.

Their society had been burdened with a generation of young women of marriageable age, and no male counterparts to marry. Likewise, so they'd been told, there was a world with a population of young eligible werewolf males without females to wed and, supposedly, they were even *more* eager to meet. The Conscriptor had stressed the word "eager" in a way that made some of the girls giggle and exchange bright-eyed looks of delight. Others were more outwardly reserved, even if they were just as titillated by the suggestive inference.

As recently as a fortnight before, the young ladies had never heard of werewolves. The description of their species was a little horrifying at first, but desperation overrode choosiness and they decided they were willing to take a look. By the time the day of arrival came, all reservations had melted into a breathless anticipation.

Lessie wore a yellow dress that complemented her auburn-streaked hair and light brown eyes. Set against the bright sunshine of the morning, the color almost made her appear to glow, as if she was walking surrounded by a halo.

The wolves were arriving on the docks by an

ocean that was sparkling with reflected sunlight. The means of their arrival was nothing less than dazzling to humans who were accustomed to ordinary, mundane lives.

From the hillside Lessie and her friends could see the prospective husbands come into view one at a time, as if they were walking out of nothingness and taking form as they emerged. It seemed to the girls that it was a god-like thing to do, appearing out of nowhere. That, of course, added to their mystique and made the occasion even more thrilling. The prospects were arriving quickly enough to become a group and be scoping out their surroundings by the time the bachelorettes reached the dock en masse.

The werewolves had been told they would have their work cut out for them if they wanted to convince a human female to commit to mate and leave her home forever. With that in mind, they had studied what behaviors women find attractive in men, along with actual classes in the arts of love, taught by a sex demon who was a friend of their alpha. They had come to the land of brides prepared for pursuit of a mate to be the challenge of their lives. So the last thing they expected was to be, more or less, besieged by a crowd of beauties in brightly colored dresses and brighter smiles that conveyed receptiveness to social advances.

Lessie's friends had rushed into the crowd of wolves with an enthusiasm that she found embarrassing. She'd hung back at the edge of the throng, feeling and, perhaps, looking uncertain.

While she was trying to decide whether she would continue to observe or join the mixer, the air dazzled a few feet away and she was face to face with a male who simply and literally took her breath away. He was a little taller than she, with golden skin and long mahogany-colored hair worn loose down his back. But the single feature that caught her attention so that she couldn't have looked away, not even if she was on fire, was his eyes. His irises were a gray so pale they made him seem even more alien than she'd been expecting. But the otherworldly look of his eyes was softened and warmed when the edges of his mouth turned up into a wolf smile.

As it happened, he seemed to be just as capti-vated by her and never took his eyes away. Relations with the opposite sex were both easy and natural for werewolves as they were sexual creatures with an innate charismatic appeal, particularly where humans were concerned. One look at the face of the prey who had wandered into his path told the wolf that his pursuit could be both fruitful and rewarding beyond his dreams.

"What's your name?" asked the wolf.

"Lestriv," said the girl.

"Lestriv." He repeated her name slowly as if he was tasting it and rolling it around on his tongue. "That's hard to say." His conclusion was offered with a teasing smile that made his eyes light from within.

She resisted the impulse to reach out and trace the strong pronounced line of his jaw with her fingertips, but just barely. Instead she returned his smile, feeling shy about her inexperience with the opposite sex and, at the same time, emboldened by his obvious interest.

"I guess that's why most people call me Lessie."

He tried out "Lessie" the same way and, looking satisfied, said, "Much better."

The werewolf took a step toward her. She took a step back reflexively, not because she wanted to retreat from him. She didn't. It was simply an involuntary response.

She couldn't have known it, but it was the best thing she could have done if she wanted to snag a wolf because that small response awakened his predatory instincts and made her an object of even greater fascination.

"Don't be afraid," said the wolf.

"I'm… not," Lessie stumbled.

"I'll not harm you. In fact," his mouth curled in a way that made her knees weak, "I'll show you more pleasure than you've ever imagined. If you'll let me."

At that he reached out at arm's length and ran a warm finger down her cheek. She couldn't suppress a shiver. He couldn't stop his smile from widening when he saw it.

Inside she might have been contemplating the many ways she would like to explore his claim of commanding pleasure, but what her mouth said was, "What's your name?"

He raised his chin and offered a charming little lopsided grin. "Jimmy Clear Eyes."

Lessie cocked her head to the side and studied him. "That suits you fine, werewolf."

Again, he took a step toward the woman. This time she did not back away.

"*You* suit me fine, human."

THE SOUND OF wind chimes blown by sweet sunny breezes stopped abruptly as Lessie started to feel the corporeal weight of her body waking. She heard a woman's voice repeat, "They're here," but it wasn't Elise announcing Jimmy's arrival. It was the alpha's mate, Luna, come to help get her ready for the worst day of her life, Jimmy's funeral.

Inside her mind chanted, "No," over and over again, as though she could use the word as a shield against reentering the nightmare of her reality. But she couldn't hold wakefulness at bay forever.

New tears sprang into eyes badly swollen from crying for two days. As she turned in the bed, her hand automatically went to her belly, which was just beginning to show the world that their second child was seeded and growing. She hoped that the baby, he or she, was insulated from sharing the pain in her heart.

Jimmy.

CHAPTER 2

✗

Earlier.

THE WOLVES OF Lunark Dimension had come to think of their world as the closest thing to paradise on the waking side of fantasy. The human mates who were part of the Elk Mountain Tribe agreed. The werewolves who had migrated from harsher climates appreciated the mild weather as well as the lush landscape, the plentiful game, and the quiet serenity of old ways where the loudest noise ever heard was a wolf howl or the squawk of a blue jay.

The three tribes had learned not only to live peaceably with each other, but to work together for the good of future generations. No small accomplishment for hot headed, territorial werewolves, but they managed to set aside the contentious side of their natures in favor of a better future for everyone. And all was well until *they* came.

The dragon shifters.

They didn't ask the original inhabitants of First Colony, led by the alpha, SilverRuff, for permission. They simply saw an opportunity and took it.

Like werewolves, dragon shifters had run out of hospitable places. Unlike werewolves, the dragon shifters were to blame for being hunted to extinction. They left destruction, often needless destruction, and massive loss of life wherever they went. They didn't just kill for survival. Like domesticated cats, they often killed for a perverse view of fun.

For werewolves, killing without need was tantamount to sacrilege.

Over the centuries, human resistance to dragons had evolved from spears to arrows to drones, which meant that humans climbed past the dragon shifters on the power chain by perfecting artificial, but dramatically superior wings, claws, and fangs. And their radar was more sophisticated than any engineered by nature.

The Lunark werewolves had only spears and arrows. They were determined that there would be a planetary ban on any device with gunpowder or a computer chip, anything that demanded large amounts of unnaturally generated power. It was a law designed to protect their beautiful wilderness and the old ways in perpetuity, but as it turned out, it might also be their undoing.

HUNTERS BEGAN TO report to their respective alphas, SilverRuff, Stalkson Grey and Liulf, that game carcasses had been picked over or simply left to rot in open fields. Worse, the dragon shifters were building a fortress type dwelling on the stone face peak of the highest mountain, high above the tree line. That vantage point would give the dragon shifters a full turn view for miles around.

SilverRuff, alpha of the original Lunark colony, had founded an intertribal Council after she'd given permission for two other werewolf tribes to migrate to Lunark. Each territory was represented by the alpha, two seconds, and two pack elders.

The Council normally met on the first day of the new moon every month. They would certainly have called an emergency meeting had it not been for the fact that the new moon was only a day after alarming reports began to come in.

Liulf, alpha of the New Scotia Pack, had two brothers who stood as his seconds. Konochur, and Cenead, informally known as Conn and Ken. On the day of the new moon, they had human hands strap packs onto their wolf forms carrying clothes they would wear to the Council meeting. In their case, kilts, boots, and long sleeve Henley type shirts made from locally grown hemp.

Council meetings were typically more social than business. Once they had decided that unity was a good thing, the werewolves took to cooperation and compromise as an extension of the core social animal that they were and quickly came to value and appreciate goals and policies that served the entire population, not just their tribe.

On that particular new moon, the mood was somber and serious as the discussion at hand.

Liulf's own mate, Rain Falling, occupied a unique position. She was mate to the alpha of the New Scotia Pack and daughter to SilverRuff, alpha of the First Colony pack. She had been one of SilverRuff's seconds before mating Liulf, and chose to retain her rank as second to the First Colony contingent. To date that had not presented a problem, but Liulf recognized that being on opposite sides of an issue could make for an interesting dynamic in his home.

Rain Falling was incensed that the dragon shifters had taken up residence without asking her mother's permission, and was so impassioned that she stood to begin the discussion.

"It's not just a matter of disrespecting my mother. It's a flagrant challenge to all of us, everyone who lives on Lunark. *All* shifters, even bloody dragons, know better than to do such a thing. And that can only mean that they are being deliberately provocative. They want a war."

Her passion was contagious and her words were followed by murmurs of agreement throughout the tent. Everyone waited to see who would speak next. After a time, Ken stood. All the wolves waited for him to speak with a concentrated focus. Ken was known for his keen mind and his inventive approach to problems. He didn't send waves of alpha power ahead of his speech, although he could have. His philosophy was something along the lines of *let those named alpha be alpha.*

"I'm wonderin' if we might no' try a diplomatic mission." There was a moment of stunned silence followed by a din that rose as wolves turned to their neighbors to give their first reaction to the outrageous idea. Ken waited patiently for quiet, then added, "Before we go off half-cocked."

"I never go anywhere *half*-cocked," shouted BigTooth, who was SilverRuff's other second. To be sure everyone got his joke, BigTooth grabbed his package and gave it a shake for emphasis.

Everyone laughed, which Ken appreciated, because it relieved some of the tension.

Again Ken waited until the laughter had died down before continuing.

"I know 'tis no' a typical notion for werewolves, but we're formin' a new way of bein' here. If we can avoid a war with dragon shifters, 'tis in our best interest to do so. I'm no' sayin' we can no' win such a conflict, but we can no' win without givin' up some of the thin's about our way of life that we hold dearest."

The room went perfectly quiet and still because everyone present understood exactly what

Ken meant. After a few minutes of silence, Stalkson Grey stood up.

"My nephew by marriage makes the kind of good sense we've come to expect from him. And we can't ignore it. If we can persuade the dragon shifters to live with us peacefully and follow a few rules regarding the hunting of game, that would be the best outcome by far. None of us wants to contemplate what going to war with dragons would mean to our way of life."

As Stalkson Grey sat down, there were hushed murmurs as wolves whispered to those near them.

Next, SilverRuff stood. "I agree with everything that's been said. It's true that diplomacy is outside typical consideration of options when it comes to strategy. But as both Ken and Grey have suggested, in this case, we have *a lot* to lose. I propose that we make Ken head of an exploratory mission, the object of which is to find out if the dragons are amenable to living in harmony. I propose that he take a contingent of six werewolves, two from each tribe, to accompany him and report back to the alphas."

SilverRuff sat down. BigTooth said, "Will there be any more discussion before we call for a vote?"

When no one answered, BigTooth called for the vote. There were eleven for and four against.

SilverRuff stood again. "Ken. Do you accept a Council commission to lead a group to the dragons and learn their intentions?"

Ken stood. "Aye. I'll go."

SilverRuff nodded. "In that case, I think you should be the one to choose who will accompany you. Two from each tribe. You'll go day after tomorrow. This Council will reconvene the day after that to reevaluate our position based on the results."

KEN HAD GOTTEN to know wolves from other tribes at the fire festivals and had no trouble choosing. Before the Council dispersed, he told SilverRuff and Stalkson Grey which two representatives from their tribes were being drafted for the mission. He specified the place and hour where they would rendezvous and everyone was agreed.

Truthfully, most of the Council members left with little hope that Ken's idea would be successful and preserve their corner of paradise, but each had a glimmer of hope that it would work. With so much at stake, the least they could ask of themselves was to keep an open mind.

TWO DAYS AFTER the Council meeting, seven wolves emerged where verdant forest met barren stone near the top of the Lost Sky mountain range. The rapidity with which the fortress was taking shape was impressive. It was also daunting and clearly meant to be intimidating. It sent a message. The dragons intended to claim the mountain as their own.

Ken's group was met by several large men whom they presumed to be shifters. The wolves quickly changed to human form and greeted the newcomers cordially. SilverRuff had named Ken leader partly because it was his idea, but she'd also learned to respect his keen intellect and even temper. She knew that, if a cool head became necessary, Liulf's younger brother was a good bet.

Ken stepped forward and motioned to the other wolves. "We've noticed that we have new neighbors. 'Tis quite a structure ye've begun." Ken glanced upward to indicate the rock face outcropping. The men stared at Ken and the other wolves in silence, without perceivable expression. "I'm sure 'tis a spectacular view."

One of the men murmured something to the one standing in the forefront. The leader-apparent raised his chin and said, "Is that Scot we hear?"

"Aye. Like ye, I'm no' a native. I'm Cenead, New Scotia Pack."

"We don't like Scots."

Ken could have taken offense, but chose to give diplomacy a chance. He chuckled, but didn't look away. "Well, I'm sure ye have yer reasons. Perhaps Scots do no' care for ye either?" Ken let that thought sit for a moment before proceeding. "'Tis a reason why we've climbed so high this mornin'. The alphas of the three tribes that have settled here *before* ye wish to extend an invitation to meet."

The apparent leader smirked at that while the men with him engaged in a mix of laughter and sneering.

The wolves had heard plenty of stories about dragon shifters before, but none had ever been close to one in the flesh. It seemed that, when the dragons shifted to two leg form, they retained surprising aspects of their animal's nature.

First, they had vertical pupils, which was

unsettling, particularly so on a two legged creature. Second, when they opened their mouths to laugh, they revealed teeth that came to sharp points.

Ken could see it wasn't going to go as they'd hoped.

"Shall we take that to mean ye have no interest in our hospitality? Would ye at least care to give a name?"

"Why would we want to become friendly with food?"

Ken suspected that he was unable to keep the look of shock from his face. He heard the changes in breathing of the wolves who stood behind him and knew that they had been baited, as a group, by that outrageously provocative statement.

A suggestion that shifters, even those of different species, might eat one another was so abhorrent, it was simply unthinkable.

"'Tis how you want to be leavin' thin's between us?"

"Tell you what. If you and the mongrels with you, can reach the bottom of the mountain before we catch you, we might decide to be good sports and choose something else for dinner."

The other dragon shifters laughed at that.

With nothing left to be said, Ken shifted to wolf form. Determined to leave with dignity intact, he turned and trotted unhurriedly back to the safety of forest, with the others in the small contingent following. When they reached the bottom of the mountain, Ken shifted to human form so that he could speak.

"Just in case they were no' playin' games, we're waitin' here in the trees for cover of darkness. If we start across the open areas when 'tis still light, they could take us and there'd be nothin' we could do about it. The moon is new. 'Tis still dark when the sun sets and the dragons will no' hunt then. They can no' see as well as we can in darkness. Then we go to our respective tribes and tell our alphas what we've seen and heard."

"Tell your alphas that I requested that each of you attend the Council meeting, just in case the members have questions and want to hear yer impressions."

The seven took wolf form, curling into each other for warmth and comfort. Feeling relatively safe under the cover of forest, they napped the rest of the afternoon away.

Ken woke to the sound of a howl. It was dark and their families were very likely getting worried.

He poked each wolf with his nose and then dashed out of the woods in the direction of New Scotia. Two followed. Two more headed in the direction of First Colony and the remaining two streaked for New Elk Mountain.

CHAPTER 3

✖

THE DIPLOMATIC SCOUTS made their reports to their alphas and, as SilverRuff had declared, the Council met again the day after. The discussion on whether or not to overturn Lunark's policy on technology, particularly arms, was far from consensus. The first day was a volley of raised voices. By the second day, everyone who had something to say had been given the opportunity to speak and talks were devolving into heated argument, fueled by the resistance of the First Colony contingent.

Liulf had been silent for the duration, carefully listening to the various points of view, trying to evaluate each on its own merit. By the afternoon of the second day, he was ready to add his opinion. When he stood, voices quieted immediately. He was not only one of three alphas who carried immense respect and authority, but also an imposing figure even among creatures as impressive as werewolves.

He addressed the First Colonists directly.

"I have heard yer speeches and know that each of ye speaks from the heart. I understand why ye feel as ye do.

"When I first visited this world, I recognized it for the paradise that it was. No one of sound mind would argue that the old ways are no' better for our kind, me least of all. If I could choose anythin', I would choose to have Lunark forever remain as it *has* been.

"Perhaps the dragons' threats were a strange form of jest that we don't understand." He glanced at Ken, who met his gaze and gave Liulf a subtle, but distinct shake of his head. "But 'tis no' likely. My brother, Ken, has a gift for true observation and I've good reason to trust his judgment. If he says the dragons are a serious and imminent danger to us, I believe him. And I believe we need to prepare to protect our tribes. This is said to ye by one who has spent much of the past millennium defendin' territory from invaders.

"SilverRuff's tribe has ne'er lived with human technology. For First Colony, 'tis an unknown."

He looked at the First Colony wolves, eyes lingering on his mate for a second longer than the others. "Suspicion and reluctance is natural and warranted. The rest of us know that, like most thin's, there's good and bad. I also know that muscle, fang, and claw will no' protect my mate and my tribe from this threat. Likewise, bow and arrow will no' bring down dragons."

Liulf paused for a full minute as he looked around the room. "'Tis my job as alpha to protect those who have put their faith in me, old, young, wee, and strong. All count on me, as they do the other alphas and elders.

"We did no' ask for this. Far from it. We would all like to have thin's remain as they were. But when dragons migrate to Lunark without permission and refer to our emissaries as food, we are left with no choice but to prepare the best defense possible. If that means acquirin' advanced weaponry from off-world," he pursed his lips for a moment, "I say aye."

As Liulf moved to sit down, the representatives from New Scotia and New Elk Mountain responded with howls and shouts and pounded the tables in front of them with their hands.

The members from First Colony remained

silently sullen. One of their elders had just begun to rise to make a response, when two Elk Mountain wolves charged into the tent, changing to human form as they arrived. One tried to begin speaking before his snout had finished retracting and re-forming into a human nose and mouth. He was clearly frustrated by his garbled speech. He growled and shook his head violently as if that would speed up his transformation.

Stalkson Grey had moved toward the new arrivals at first alarm. "Redmane. What brings you here looking like a devil is chasing you?"

After a few more seconds, Redmane's words became intelligible. "Seven of us were stalking game on the foothills. The dragons came." He was panting, still out of breath. "When we saw them we tried to run, but... they flew close enough to the earth to slash at us with their tails." He stopped and looked into Grey's darkening eyes. "It was like they were playing with us. When they flew away, three hunters were dead."

Stalkson Grey straightened. "Who?"

"Cloudspring. Pathmaker. Jimmy Clear Eyes. Three of our best." Redmane looked down at the ground. "All had families."

"Have they been told?"

Redmane glanced up at his alpha, but his eyes went immediately back to the ground in front of him. "No, Alpha. The widows don't know."

"Go outside and wait for me." After the two wolves were outside, Stalkson Grey turned back to the Council. "As you've heard, I'm needed. If anything useful could come from the senseless deaths of young wolves, let it be that you make the right decision. We need weapons powerful enough to either exterminate the dragons or persuade them to move on to another world. The New Elk Mountain tribe votes yes. As you are deciding, remember that I'm leaving to attend to our dead and the loved ones left behind by this senseless act."

As Grey turned to leave he heard one of the First Colony advisors tell SilverRuff that he had warned her the whole Council thing was a mistake. With that the wolves from Grey's tribe departed for the grim rituals of informing families and arranging funeral rites.

The remaining assembly fell silent for a time after the Elk Mountain wolves were gone. They were, no doubt, each in their own way, contemplating the implications of Lunark werewolves being murdered without provocation.

Liulf and Ken leaned together in a whisper a few seconds before Ken rose and called for a vote.

"As ye all heard, New Elk Mountain votes aye. Likewise, New Scotia says aye."

There was an immediate uproar as the infuriated First Colony contingent rose to their feet. SilverRuff, while remaining seated, simply raised a hand. Her confidantes begrudgingly took their seats and waited for her to speak.

"We agreed when the Council was formed that a majority vote would win. Two out of three tribes have voted to import weaponry sufficient to eliminate the threat, now confirmed, posed by the dragon shifters. First Colony will honor the vote and abide by the terms of the Council," she looked pointedly to her right and left at the other First Colonists, "as agreed.

"According to the plan set out by Stalkson Grey, we will await an off-world visitor who might convey our need to those who would give us aid. In the meantime, the young must be always attended and always close to shelter. Hunt and travel only at night. We must exercise great caution if we want to contain the damage.

Naturally all Gatherings are suspended until the threat is resolved.

"Anything else?" She looked around the room at the remaining Council members. No one moved or indicated that they had something to add. "We are adjourned. Wait until dark. Carry this news to your tribes.

"Liulf." Liulf raised his chin when SilverRuff spoke to him directly. "Please send a messenger to your uncle with the news of this decision."

Liulf nodded once, then leaned over and murmured something to Ken, who, likewise nodded.

CHAPTER 4

✕

S TALKSON GREY COULDN'T remember a
funeral burdened by such a great sorrow.
Three very young werewolves struck down
before they'd passed so much as a single century.
As the one responsible for the migration to
Lunark, there was an ugly voice in his head
repeatedly suggesting that he was to blame for
the disaster. The task of carrying the news to the
families had been gut-wrenching, easily the
hardest task he'd *ever* been called on to perform
as a duty of the alpha.

The first day, the bodies of the slain were
cleaned and wrapped. The second day the
families sat in the room with them while
members of the pack came to offer condolences.
All the while they could hear the sounds of the
pyre being built.

On the third night the widows and children

were brought to the pyre. The alpha's wife, Luna, was responsible for escorting Lestriv, mate to Jimmy Clear Eyes. Through Lestriv's haze of grief, she was still able to recognize the enormous assembly who had come to pay their respects to the fallen. Many of those present were from First Colony and New Scotia, including Liulf and his brothers, Konochur and Cenead. That meant many faces she'd never seen since she'd never been to one of the Gatherings. Jimmy wasn't interested or curious. He'd been happy to be at home with his girls and she'd been happy to be at home with him.

Songs were sung to help speed the spirits of the dead onward to a happy place with blue sky, clear water, green grass, tall trees, and no natural enemies. At the appropriate time, Stalkson Grey came forward and said the ancient words of mourning.

The number and ages of the victims made it the most solemn occasion that Konochur had ever witnessed. The sorrow hanging in the air was palpable. When his uncle finished reciting the poem of spirit flight, he lit three torches, and gave one to each of the widows as it was custom to have surviving mates light the pyre.

That was the first time Conn had ever laid eyes on Lestriv.

She didn't hang her head and weep like the other two. She threw the torch with resolution, then stepped back and stared at the rising flames while streams of stoically silent tears coursed down her cheeks and fell on her breast.

Conn's heart squeezed in his chest as he watched her, transfixed. Without taking her eyes away from the flames that reached toward the sky, Lestriv bent and lifted a little girl who clung to her skirt. His eyes drifted downward to the slight swell of her belly and a renewed sense of outrage washed over him.

It was well known that Conn had never had much use for humans and had never understood why a wolf would stoop to mate with one. But truth be told, Conn had never understood why anyone would mate at all when there was so much sexual variety to be experienced. That was why it surprised him so when the voice in his head chanted, "'Tis no' right to be a widow so young and for no good reason."

When the attendees began to file away, the three brothers remained to speak to their uncle about the plans to arm. Liulf asked Grey to be informed about any new development.

"I will, of course. You're welcome to stay with us until tomorrow night." He gestured toward the three.

"Nay, Uncle, if we go now, we'll be in New Scotia when the moon is still high."

Grey nodded. "I believe it meant a lot to the families that you came and I thank you on their behalf."

"No need. We're all in it together." As an afterthought, he added, "Good times and bad."

"Just so, Liulf," Grey said.

AFTER A FEW days of thinking about the widow and a few restless night's sleep, Conn decided it was time to pay his uncle's village a visit. When he arrived, he didn't go straight to see Stalkson Grey, but wandered around until he spotted Lessie. She was hanging clothes up to dry on the side of a small cabin. He observed her for a while without making himself known. After she finished the hanging, she picked up the little girl he'd seen at the funeral rites, swung her around once and then stood swaying while she sang a song that was as soothing as a lullaby. The wolf was captivated by the sound of the woman's voice. It pulled him nearer like a magnet and did funny fluttery things to his stomach.

When the woman went inside her little cottage and closed the door, Conn went straight to his uncle's house to find the alpha's wife. He was told she was at her clinic and there he found her looking in the mouth of a wolf cub who, apparently, was too frightened of seeing the healer to hold his human form.

"Conn. What are you doing here?" Luna was clearly surprised by the visit, but pleased as well as she liked her husband's nephew-by-marriage well enough.

"I want ye to introduce me to someone."

Luna looked confused and shook her head. "Someone? What do you mean someone?" Then his meaning seemed to dawn on her and she responded with a throaty laugh that originated in her chest. That had always been one of the things Conn appreciated most about Luna. She had an unapologetically lusty laugh. "Conn," she began, shaking her head again, this time in disbelief. "I wouldn't *introduce* you to my worst enemy." She stopped what she was doing with the child and took a good look at Conn, who appeared to be both surprised and insulted. "Since when do you need introductions anyway? That doesn't sound like your style."

"Well, 'tis no'. Usually." She noted he seemed a little uncomfortable. "But this particular person might no' appreciate a simple wink and grab. She's, ah, human."

Luna's laughter started all over again. "Oh. That is too rich. Aren't you the werewolf who holds humans in complete disdain?"

Conn's eyebrows drew together. "Is that what ye think? I do no' hold *you* in disdain."

"Uh huh," she said without conviction. "So that makes me and one other. Who is it?"

Seeing that Conn looked like he was in pain, Luna began to take him a little more seriously.

"The widow. The red-haired one with the little girl."

Luna gaped at Conn for a full minute before returning to her patient. She finished with the little wolf, set him down on his feet, and sent him on his way.

"Conn, the woman you're talking about is the *last* person in this dimension that I would introduce you to."

It was Conn's turn to gape. "Why so mean, Aunt? I have no plans to brin' harm to the woman."

Luna shifted her weight to one side and put a hand on her hip in a posture of challenge. "What then? You're going to offer to mate her?"

Since the day Luna had learned that werewolves are real creatures, she had never been as surprised as she was by Conn's hesitation in answering that question. He seemed to be searching for the right thing to say. Awkwardly.

"Well," he stumbled, "I'm no' sayin' that exactly."

"Then what are you saying? *Exactly.*"

"That I'd like to get to know her better." He tried for a nonchalant shrug.

"Know her better," Luna said drily. "That's what I thought."

"'Tis *no'* what I meant, Luna. You're twistin' my meanin'. I did no' mean gettin' to know her better in a *carnal* sort of way." Luna looked unconvinced. "Exactly."

"Since when have you had any interest in females other than in a carnal sort of way, wolf?" Luna smirked.

Conn screwed up his face with a mix of expressions from frustration to aggravation of the most perplexed sort. "For Spirit's sake, human.

I'll just do this myself."

Luna grew serious. "You will not do any such thing, Conn. She's had enough torment at her doorstep without having to deal with a horndog wolf dry humping the door jamb."

He was clearly confused. "I do no' know what a horndog is, but if I take yer meanin', 'tis no' as complimentary as I'd like. That aside, I can see that 'twas wrong to ask for help here. So I'll just be on my way."

Luna narrowed her eyes. "Very well. Just make sure that 'on your way' you don't pass by the widow's house."

Conn gave her a glare and started for the open doorway. Luna hurried round and stepped in front of him. "I'll be needing your word, Conn. That you will leave her alone."

Conn towered over Luna when he stepped closer, but she didn't give way. "I'll be needin' you to step away from the door, Luna."

Luna blocked the door with her arms. "Promise me."

"Are you movin' away from the door?"

"Not until you promise you will leave the widow alone."

"Can ye be dissuaded from this course?"

"No," Luna said firmly, her chin in the air.

CONN WATCHED AS Lestriv sat her little girl by the entrance to the chicken pen. With a wicker basket over her arm she began struggling to open the gate. It was mostly mesh, but framed and supported with heavy posts made from four inch tree trunks. One of the hinges had loosened in such a way as to make the gate unwieldy and hard to manage.

Lessie jumped when she heard a voice close behind her. It was deep, but soft and pleasant, and gave no cause for alarm.

"Here. Let me help with that."

She turned to look directly up into Conn's face and immediately blushed, partly because of the thought that he was sexy, beautiful and charismatically compelling, and partly from guilt for noticing that just a week after her husband's funeral. When Conn reached past her to take hold of the gate, she stepped back, but not before he noticed that her scent was intoxicating as peach trumpet vine. He took a deep whiff.

"What are you doing?" she asked.

"Hmmm? Oh, no' a thin'. What's yer name?" he asked.

She looked around, wiping her hands on her apron. "Lestriv," she said without looking at him.

He repeated her name slowly, then smiled. "'Tis hard to say."

Conn thought he saw surprise on her face as her eyes jerked to his. That was just before she seemed to get a faraway look like she was no longer actually seeing him.

"Lestriv?"

He watched her face and she refocused her attention on him, on the here and now. "People usually call me Lessie."

"Ah. Much better. And what's yer name?" He looked at the little girl and smiled. She was a beautiful child with mahogany-colored hair and eyes the same gray color as the skies of his homeland in northern Scotia.

The child didn't react to him or answer until her mother prompted her. "Say your name, love."

"Lileeee."

Conn smiled.

"Her father named her Liluye. It means 'hawk singing while soaring'. We call her Lily and she just turned four."

Conn looked down at the child. "Hello, Lily.

I'm Conn." He looked at Lessie. "Well, actually 'tis Konuchur, but most people call me Conn and I'd like it if ye would as well." As an afterthought he decided to add his credentials. "I'm second to the alpha of New Scotia."

"I know who you are."

"Do ye?" Conn seemed surprised.

Lessie smiled a little. "Everyone, well, at least all the females know who you are. Your reputation is, um, well-known?" Conn looked away and began fiddling with the misbehaving hinge. Lessie thought she saw a red flush touch his cheeks. "What does Konuchur mean?"

Conn turned his face away and mumbled something.

"I'm sorry. I didn't understand."

When he turned toward her, Lessie could see that she was right about the fact that his face was flushed. He appeared to be nervous and fidgety. "Wolf lover," he said under his breath.

Lessie stared for a moment and then chuckled. "Of course."

"I'm goin' to need to go get some tools to fix this. I can prop it open so you can get inside and will be back before ye're ready to go."

"Alright. You don't have to do this though. I

can get someone to fix it."

"I'm someone," Conn countered.

"Well, of course, you are." Lestriv was blushing again and her hands were fluttering nervously. "I meant one of the men who live here."

The lie spilled out without having been thought through as well as it could have been. "Actually I've been assigned by the Council to look after ye and make sure that ye have everythin' ye need. Ye and yer family." He glanced at Lily.

Lessie shifted her weight back on her heels. "That was very thoughtful of them, but I'm not sure we…" She looked down at Lily.

"Do no' give it a care. I'm happy to do what I can."

Lessie opened her mouth to say something, but Conn wrenched open the gate with brute force. "In ye go before the chicks take to the hills." She grabbed Lily's hand and the two of them stepped inside. "Back in a few minutes."

Lessie nodded and gave him a small, shy smile. "Alright."

True to his word, Conn was back with tools before Lessie had finished gathering eggs. She was alternating between watching Lily play and watching Conn work on the hinge, when she heard a deafening roar and looked up to see the alpha, Stalkson Grey, bearing down on Conn with rage written all over his face and posture.

When Lessie married Jimmy Clear Eyes, Stalkson Grey became her alpha as well. She had no fear of him because she knew him to be both fair and kind, but she had also seen enough to know that an infuriated alpha is a very bad thing.

To his credit, or his foolishness, Conn did not step back when his uncle stopped within inches of his face. "Uncle," Conn acknowledged with casual simplicity and a calm that seemed entirely out of keeping with the situation. He held the alpha's gaze and refused to look away, which Lessie took as an indication that Conn was ready to die.

Stalkson Grey was seething. "Before I rip the throat from your neck, would you care to explain why you left my mate tied to a chair?"

"Aye. We had a disagreement. One that could no' be resolved otherwise." Grey's eyes went wide at the audacity of Conn's response. "I had no' wish to hurt her, and would ne'er do so, o' course, but she had set herself against my purpose and was refusin' to allow me through the door."

Grey blinked three times. "You're saying that my mate attempted to prevent your departure from the clinic? Why would she do that?"

Conn glanced toward Lestriv. "Because she disagreed with the Council's decision to assign me as the widow's caretaker, in her husband's absence."

Grey shook his head in confusion. "She…"

It was then that Grey noticed Lessie holding a basket of eggs and anxiously observing the exchange. Grey turned back to Conn whose eyes were silently pleading with his uncle to not blow his cover. Grey's face softened when he recognized the mate fever written all over his nephew.

The alpha quickly turned his back on the chicken coop because he knew he could suppress outright laughter with enough exercise of will, but would not be able to stop the smile pulled at his mouth over Conn's predicament. Conn looked aloof on the outside, but was a bundle of nerves within as he waited for his uncle to finish whatever he was doing with his back turned.

When Grey swung around, he nodded to Lessie, acknowledging her presence for the first time. She said, "It was very nice of the Council to make sure that Lily and I are taken care of. I know we haven't had a chance to talk about it since…" She trailed off as if she couldn't finish that thought. "But I suppose I could go back home, since Jimmy is… gone."

Grey looked at Lestriv with such compassion. He'd been a widower himself and knew a thing or two about grief and being left with a child to raise. He'd also been lucky enough to get a second chance at love and hoped that Lessie would have the same good fortune.

"Of course we want you to stay with us, Lessie. This is your home. You're as much a part of the tribe as anyone here."

Lestriv was genuinely honored by that simple speech. "Thank you, Alpha."

"As far as the Council assigning Conn to look after you," he glanced at Conn, who was shaking his head slightly with an expression so pained it looked like he was having a heart attack, "I agree that it was a nice idea." Conn let out the breath he was holding in a whoosh of relief that made Grey smile again. To Conn he said, "I'll give your aunt your profound apologies," he said pointedly, "and make explanations. I know for a fact that she's forgiving about desperation."

"Thank ye, Uncle."

"I guess we'll be seeing a lot of you?"

Conn almost beamed. "I suspect so."

"Good day, Lessie."

"Good day, Alpha."

Conn turned to Lessie and smiled looking confident and at ease for the first time since he'd arrived at the chicken pen. After a few minutes he had the hinge working properly and tested the gate by letting it swing back and forth a few times. One of the hens, who apparently didn't know the difference between a human and a werewolf, tried to get through the gate. Conn swooped her up in a blur of movement and threw her into the air so that she flew for a few seconds before lighting in the middle of the pen. Lily let out a delighted squeal followed by a heart-melting series of giggles.

Conn grinned at her. "Want to see it again?"

Lily nodded enthusiastically and showed off a grin that was missing a tooth.

For the next half hour, Conn gave the hens the thrill of a few seconds of flight, while Lily and her mother laughed. He treasured that laughter, embedding the sound deep in his heart, and thought that curbing the widow's sadness, even for a short while, far overshadowed the usefulness of fixing the chicken coop gate.

Conn insisted on carrying both the eggs and Lily on the walk back to the cottage. "Is there something else around the house that I might do while I'm here?"

"No," Lessie shook her head and smiled politely. "We're fine." She turned toward the door, but hesitated and turned back again. "I've had an elk stew simmering on the hearth since this morning. If you'd like to join us for midday meal? Before you start home?"

Conn was about ten inches taller than Lessie. As he looked down at her, he had the errant thought that ten inches was probably the perfect difference in height between a wolf and his mate. "I'd be honored if ye're certain there's enough."

"There's plenty," Lessie said.

THE COTTAGE WAS small and humble, but comforting in its homey rusticity. It also had that elusive factor, a sense of harmonious energy. It was a sense that the occupants loved each other and that arguments were rare.

The stew was to Conn's liking. When he

reached for the salt, Lessie smiled.

"What?"

"Jimmy liked a lot of salt on his food. Maybe werewolves like more salt than humans."

"Maybe. We're lucky to have the great salt plain on the other side of the mountain range. 'Tis big enough to keep all the tribes satisfied. There will no' be any salt wars here."

"Salt wars," she said. "Sounds so silly compared to dragon wars."

Conn put down his spoon and said slowly, "We have a plan. They will no' be here much longer." His gaze locked on Lessie's eyes. "Do ye want to tell me about him?"

"Him? Jimmy?"

Conn nodded.

"Well," she smiled sadly, "you know the story about how the young wolves without mates came bride-shopping to my world." She looked away like she was remembering a happy time. "I guess I fell for Jimmy the instant I saw him. I was the first girl he saw. Literally. And I guess I was lucky that he didn't just nod and keep looking. For something better."

Conn wanted to interrupt and assure her that there was no such thing as 'something better', but he kept quiet.

"He was my first and only romance. We had a good life and I never thought that I'd be the one lighting a torch to his pyre. He was the one who was practically immortal." Conn noticed that her eyes had glazed over and that she was absently tracing circles on her belly. When her eyes refocused, she said, "I'm pregnant. I don't know if you knew that."

Conn nodded. "I guessed as much. 'Tis hard to keep secrets from werewolves. We notice details, if no' with our eyes, then with our noses. We can even smell sadness."

"You can?" She seemed amazed by that. "I wonder what that would be like."

"Has it been hard to live with wolves?"

She grinned in response. "Oh, no. Not at all. In some ways werewolf society makes more sense than human society."

"In what ways?"

She looked thoughtful while she chewed a bite of stew. When she was finished, she said, "Well, for instance, assigning someone to watch over a widow? That's pretty special."

For the first time Conn felt guilty about the lie. "I'm no' sure 'tis a common thin'. But I'm glad I'm the one privileged to make sure that the two of ye are well."

"Yes. Thank you, Conn."

"Ye're an excellent cook, Lessie. I could eat yer stew every day." And he hoped the time would come that he could prove that declaration to be true.

"Nice of you to say."

"Speakin' of food. How are yer stores?"

"Well, we have a small root cellar. The chickens are producing enough eggs for every family in our co-op to have two or three a day. We have meat packed in salt in the little building out back. Jimmy was a hunter, you know. So meat was never a problem."

"And 'twill ne'er be a problem for ye. With yer permission I'll check on that before I go." She nodded. "About the dragons, please stay close to shelter, where ye could duck in if they came. Whate'er ye do, do no' go out in the open areas. No' until the problem is resolved. And keep the wee one with ye always."

Lessie understood the deadly seriousness of the warning. "I understand." She looked at Lily. "I hope it isn't this way forever. Children should be able to play."

"Aye. They should. And they will. Just give us a little time."

CHAPTER 5

✕

DAYS TURNED INTO weeks as Stalkson Grey
patiently waited for someone from Black
Swan to show up, either for a visit or just to
check in and see how they were. On Deliverance's last visit, he'd been told that his son and
the remains of the original Elk Mountain Tribe
were close to being ready to join them. Grey had
asked Deliverance to take a message to Windwalker saying that they would be ready to reunite
the tribe and welcome them at any time. And
that he missed seeing his grandchildren.

When Deliverance dropped by to deliver the
news that Win was ready to immigrate with the
Elk Mountain werewolves, the last thing he
expected was to have Grey say that the wolves of
unarmed Lunark Dimension, needed weapons.
Heavy duty, high tech weapons and lots of them.

"Tell Win that, if they want to wait until this

problem is behind us, we'll understand. On the other hand, if they decide to come notwithstanding the dangers, we could get every one of them to carry something that could be used to obliterate that scar the dragons built on the mountaintop. We could shoot the devils from the sky and, well, that would be good."

"No love lost with the dragons then."

"The fuckers are nothing but cold-blooded thugs with big wings."

Deliverance nodded. "That's pretty much what every culture that's come in contact with them has to say. So you want me to go to Black Swan and beg for human weapons."

Stalkson Grey nodded. "If you have to."

"You know this friendship thing isn't as easy as it sounds."

"I'd do it for you."

"You would?"

"Hell yeah."

DELIVERANCE SAID GOODBYE, but before he left he decided to pay the dragon shifters his own kind of visit. The partially finished fortress was a great room, big enough for a dragon to accidentally shift indoors without bending his wings.

It had a soaring ceiling. The place looked like the aftermath of a biker party with bodies passed out wherever they fell from the party they'd had the night before. Giant tankards had rolled to a stop on the stone floor or tipped over on makeshift tables. There were females as well in various states of undress.

Deliverance climbed on top of the longest table and gave a shrill whistle. Some of the inhabitants roused to a semi-animated state. Some simply slept through. Those that were half-awake tried to pull themselves into a threatening posture.

Deliverance wasn't impressed. While he loved real dragons, he ranked dragon shifters at the bottom of the list of creatures deserving regard.

"Here's your warning, miscreants. Get yourselves sober and leave this dimension now, while you can. If you do, you'll live to trash another world. If you don't, you're going to find that you're responsible for destroying the very thing that attracted you to this world. Your choice. And let me make it easy because you don't seem that bright. Leave and live. Or stay and die."

Just as the strongest of the dragons was beginning to pull himself up, Deliverance vanished. He didn't think his speech would have any effect on the future course of the dragons, but he could feel good about trying.

WITHIN MINUTES THE demon was in Loti Dimension standing at the foot of a bed where Stalkson Grey's son, Windwalker, and his mate, Cloud, were making love. When he cleared his throat, Cloud shrieked, jerking the sheet up to cover herself while Win took Deliverance to the floor with a roar and a mid-air tackle. There was no macho satisfaction in it because the demon seemed to enjoy it. Win could tell by the laughing.

"For all that's holy, Deliverance, don't you have any understanding of propriety?" Win said as he shoved his legs into his jeans.

Deliverance shrugged, and ran his eyes over Cloud, who was scowling and grasping the covers under her chin. "Not really. I have news though. You want it or not?"

Win simply made a motion toward the door while he continued to scowl.

The demon followed Windwalker into the living room and watched the werewolf pour himself a drink. Begrudgingly, he offered the bottle to Deliverance. "It may be months before my dick unshrivels. And longer than that before Cloud feels like fucking again," he said miserably.

"Well, maybe you shouldn't be so shy."

"Has anyone ever told you that you're infuriating?"

Deliverance grinned. "Frequently. I can think of worse things."

"Like what?"

"Like not being noticed."

Windwalker sat on a leather ottoman by the hearth and stoked the embers into flame. "Okay. I'm awake now with blue balls. What's the news?"

"Your pop's got a dragon problem." Win made a circular motion with his hand to indicate that he wanted to hear more and to cut out the dramatic pauses. "You know they have a no-tech, no-gunpowder policy on Lunark. Well the dragon shifters moved in, without permission, took up residence in the mountains and proceeded to terrorize the place.

"They've left your dad and his bros no choice but to revise policy." Deliverance sat and leaned closer. "The Council sent a delegation to invite the dragons to a meet. They called werewolves food." Windwalker recoiled at that just as the members of the delegation had. "The next day the dragons killed three hunters for no reason. Just to make a show of power. Or maybe for fun. I don't know.

"Anyway, he asked me to tell you that, with the dragon thing going on, he'll understand if you want to postpone plans to join them."

Win sat in silence for a few minutes. He took a drink of Scotch and stared at the fire. "I think that, when this contingent of Elk Mountain hears that the others are in trouble, they'll want to go sooner."

Deliverance smiled. "Your dad said, just in case you leaned that way, to tell you to have every single person carry something that can be used to blast the fuckers out of the sky. Or something like that."

"I'm not following."

"He wants us to ask Black Swan for arms."

"Like what? Heat-seeking missiles."

"Well, sort of. I think heat-seeking missiles would work if you were trying to kill the dragons in human form, but if you were doing that you could just snap their necks with your jaws. If you want to kill dragons, heat-seeking won't work. They're cold blooded. Reptiles. You know?"

Win nodded. "I'm not stupid."

"I didn't say you were."

"Anybody could have made that mistake."

"Sure. None of us are arms experts."

"Right. Who is?"

"Storm."

"I know him. He came here once."

"Yeah, I know him, too. He's my son-in-law."

"No shit? Well, call him up. Let's get this show on the road."

Deliverance was a little surprised by Win's enthusiasm. "You sure you understand what I'm saying here? There's going to be ugliness. Three werewolves have already died."

"I get it, demon. Let's be quick before more are added to that number."

"Well, seems like your dick has unshriveled."

"Funny. You gonna call Storm or do you want me to?"

"Let's just go pay a visit. You want a shirt and footwear. Personally I'm not much of a fan, but I don't get cold as easily as humans."

"I'm not human."

"No offense. You know what I meant."

"No. I do not know what you meant."

"Do. You. Want. To. Go. Visit. My. Daughter's. Home. Like. That?"

Win glared at Deliverance for a few seconds, stomped toward the bedroom, and reemerged a couple of minutes later in a flannel lined denim shirt with boots on his feet.

Storm and Litha had moved back into the vineyard and were enjoying a quiet Bailey's by the fire when they heard a commotion in the kitchen.

Storm rolled his eyes.

Litha took a sip of Bailey's, then said, "It could be a burglar."

"Helloooooo," Deliverance called.

Litha looked at Storm. "Well, at least he's become semi-housebroken." She aimed her voice toward the kitchen. "IN HERE!!"

"You mean because he lands in the kitchen?" Storm snorted. "That's a far cry from even *semi*-housebroken."

It took less than ten minutes for Storm to explain that he was a *small* weapons expert and that the sort of firepower the residents of Lunark

Dimension needed was a completely different proposition. He suggested that Windwalker appeal to the Jefferson Unit Director of Research and Development, Thelonius M. Monq, and said he would call ahead, even though it would be just after midnight in New Jersey where Dr. Monq was permanently assigned.

Monq took the call from Storm, then shuffled into his office to meet with Windwalker.

He hadn't combed his hair, which made him look even more eccentric than usual. Yawning, he said, "If you'd care for coffee, I'll get one of the aides up and have him fetch."

"No, please don't," said Win. "This won't take long."

FOR THE SECOND time in a night, Windwalker Grey and the demon, Deliverance, explained what had happened on Lunark and why their appeal for large weapons was urgent.

"If I'm understanding the situation correctly," Win glanced at Deliverance, "people can't step farther than a few feet away from shelter during the daytime. Children can't play. Herdsmen can't properly care for their stock. No one can hunt or travel except at night." Win shuffled a little, huffed out a sigh, and said. "Cowering behind closed doors is not a natural state for werewolves. It doesn't sit right."

"No. I don't suppose it would. You're used to being at the top of the food chain. That aside, assuming that The Order agrees to supply your requisition, which mind you will be extremely expensive, I can make a list that should suit your needs." Monq directed his attention to the demon. "Would you be able to transport a few experts to conduct training? And bring them back, of course?"

Deliverance looked put out and flapped his hands to demonstrate that point, but agreed.

Monq looked at his watch. "In another hour, I can have a chat with headquarters in Edinburgh. Come back in, oh, say, five hours and I'll have some answers for you."

WHILE SIMON TVELGAR, Director of Black Swan Headquarters in Edinburgh, was personally sympathetic with the werewolves, he didn't think he could make a decision to exterminate a nest of dragon shifters on his sole authority.

"Are these the last of the dragons?"

"I didn't ask," replied Monq.

"Well, no matter how abominable their behavior or abhorrent they are as a species, we can't really be responsible for causing their total extinction. We would have to find a way to contain them. Perhaps lock them into a dimension from which they couldn't pass."

"Is that possible?"

"Frankly, I'm not sure. It was just a thought. Brainstorming, you know."

"So what do you intend to do?"

"Contact the Council for an up or down vote. Then we'll have to abide by whatever that is."

"Risky. The vote could be no."

There was a pause while Simon considered that. "If it is, then we'll have to relocate the werewolves to another world suitable for their needs."

"Hmmm."

"Something else you wanted to say?"

"I've been told that the werewolves have put a lot of time and energy into colonizing Lunark. They like it there and it's *their* home. Just on principle, it doesn't seem right that they should be the ones to have to move. That's the first consideration. The second is that, I'm not sure running from one world to another is any sort of solution. We could be right back here six months from now."

"I'll make a point of introducing your arguments to the discussion."

"Do what you can."

"Understood."

CHAPTER 6

✖

A S THE WEEKS went by, Konochur knocked on Lessie's door on more days than not. They fell into a relaxed, easy companionship that gave Lessie a measure of comfort. She thought about Jimmy, of course, and missed him terribly when she was alone at night in the bed they had shared. She'd left her girlhood home with him and had never thought about being on her own in the world. Why would she? She'd believed she was destined to grow old and die with a handsome young werewolf who would outlive her by centuries.

WHEN CONN, LESTRIV, and Lily neared the chicken coop, the hens set up an almost deafening cacophony of squawked greetings. Lessie turned toward Conn and said, "Seems you make a favorable impression on the girls wherever you go."

Conn gave her his most charming, most roguish, lopsided grin. "'Tis no' the chickens I'm aimin' to please. In case ye have no' figured that out by now."

Lestriv's face flushed with color, signaling that she took his meaning well enough and that she secretly admired that grin of his more than she should. Conn's way of making ordinary chores fun had penetrated her grief and brought laughter bubbling to the surface again and again. Each one of those momentary bursts of joy was followed by a pang of guilt, but it seemed she was a helpless victim of Konochur's antics.

LILY AND LESSIE laughed while the chickens backed up to Conn indicating their requests for the thrill of a few seconds of flight. They pecked at each other for a better place in line.

"Come now, ladies," Conn said. "A few seconds of joy awaits all of ye."

Afterward, as Conn watched Lessie feed the chickens, he asked, "What are ye thinkin'?"

She stopped momentarily, smiled at him, then resumed scattering feed. "That chickens dream about being eagles."

Conn gave her a hearty laugh. "Aye. Seems so." When his grin resolved to a teasing smile, he asked, "And what is it ye are dreamin' about, bonny lass?"

A frown creased her brow as she shook her head vigorously. "I have no right to be dreaming about anything, Conn. Not now."

She glanced at Konochur, who looked both serious and concerned. "'Tis no' true, Lessie. Yer mate would no' expect ye to entomb yerself in the past. Ye mated for a lifetime, but his lifetime is over. I know ye loved him. I know ye miss him. But ye have a long life ahead." He pointed toward Lily. "And much to live for."

While Lestriv had stopped dead still and was staring at the ground, Conn was kicking himself for going down that path in the middle of a chicken coop. Stalkson Grey had taken him aside and warned him that a successful courtship with a human would entail considerably more finesse than that required by werewolves. He thought he'd been prepared to go slow and be patient, but sometimes he felt like he would burst if he couldn't be honest about his intentions. He'd been relaxed and comfortable, let his guard down, and before he knew what was happening his unguarded feelings had tumbled out of his mouth.

He took a deep breath, exhaled a long sigh and said, "Lessie, forgive me. I know I do no' have the right to offer an opinion, but every creature has the right to dream." He chuckled. "Even chickens. Yer mate would no' wish to take that from ye. I know because I'm the same as he." Lestriv looked at him sharply. "I mean, I'm the same species," he added quietly.

She quickly looked down and up again. "We're finished here. Lily and I need to deliver these eggs and start supper."

Conn knew by the curt staccato of her speech that she was put off. He knew he would have to seek out his uncle's advice as to how to mend the error.

"I'll walk ye."

"There's no need, Conn. I have a few stops, but I can see the house from here."

When she picked up her basket and straightened, he put a hand on her forearm and locked her gaze to his. "I will walk ye, Lestriv." With that he took the basket of eggs from her in a gesture as courtly as any she could imagine.

By the slow deliberate way he insisted, Lessie

knew there would be no point in arguing. She was very aware that there is nothing in creation so stubborn as a werewolf whose mind is made up. So she simply took Lily's hand and started home. She kept her silence until she reached her porch, then turned and said goodbye without making eye contact.

CONN LEFT LESSIE and Lily at their door and headed straight for Grey's lodge. Since becoming Lestriv's self-appointed helper, he had practically become a resident of New Elk Mountain and, specifically, a fixture at Grey's. Luna was fairly good-natured about it and the little girls loved having him around. Luna had made some huffy remark about even babies being attracted to Conn, but once she realized he was serious about Lessie, she supported his efforts at courtship.

GREY CAUTIONED CONN about rushing and advised more patience.

"Humans are used to long periods of mourning the dead."

"Why?" Conn asked as Luna passed through the room.

"Sometimes we feel guilty about surviving.

Sometimes we just miss the departed terribly and have a hard time letting go."

After Luna had passed out of earshot, Conn said, "Maybe she just does no' like me." The glum look that had taken the place of his typical cocky smirk looked out of place on his handsome face.

Grey barked out a laugh. "My wife tells me that all the unmated females line up for a turn with you. I'm sure Lestriv likes you. Give her time. If I lost Luna, I..." He didn't finish the sentence, but his eyes glazed over as he trailed off, imagining what that might be like.

After a few moments, Conn said, "Aye, Uncle. Ye're sayin' there's no' room for me in her heart because 'tis filled with a dead wolf."

Grey focused on Conn and blinked. "Remind me never to send *you* on a diplomatic mission."

"Aye, but, how long will it be before she'll be ready to look my way?"

Grey shook his head. "There's no way to know that. Females are all different."

"I had no' noticed that so much. I mean some have rose-colored nipples and some are pink..."

Grey cut him off with a soft laugh and another shake of his head. "Sounds like you haven't spent much time getting to know them?"

"Getting to know them?" Conn repeated the question as if it was an alien concept. Grey simply walked away chuckling. "'Tis cruel of ye to find amusement in my misfortune," Conn called after him.

By the time Conn had finished having supper with his uncle's family, it was dark. He bid his goodbyes and took his time trotting home to New Scotia.

WHEN CONN DIDN'T show up at Lessie's door the next day, she began to regret having been abrupt. When he didn't come the day after that, she began examining her feelings. If she was honest with herself, she had to admit that she liked Conn and liked having him around. But that admission wasn't freeing. It was confusing. She was ashamed that she was responding to the attentions of another werewolf, when her own had only been gone a few weeks.

In her heart she pondered Conn's words regarding what Jimmy would have wanted for her. She had to agree that her mate would have wanted her to be happy, whether that chance came along sooner or later. She'd loved her mate with all her heart and part of her would always belong to him. But, she asked herself, would it be possible to love again so soon?

Jimmy hadn't just been her first love. He'd been her first everything. She'd also learned firsthand that werewolves sometimes looked at things differently. She had adjusted to the idiosyncrasies of life in wolf culture just as he had, no doubt, made compromises for her. Perhaps werewolves did mourn and move on. Perhaps she could gain some insight by talking to Luna.

She hurried through her chores and walked to the clinic with Lily after lunch. It was a relief to see that there weren't a lot of patients waiting. Just Saraf and her little boy.

"Hello, Saraf."

"Lessie." She smiled. "Is everything alright with the baby?"

Thinking that her mother's friend was talking about her, Lily said, "I'm fine. And I'm not a baby."

Saraf exchanged a smile with Lessie. "Of course you're not a baby, Lily. My mistake."

Lessie's eyes wandered to the little boy sitting on the wood bench next to Saraf. "How are you,

River? You're getting to be a big boy."

River didn't speak, but not because he couldn't. Keen intelligence shone brightly from his dark eyes. He simply chose to nod his agreement that he was, indeed, big for a four-year-old.

Luna appeared at the doorway. "Come in, Saraf." Looking over she said, "We'll be just a few minutes, Lessie."

Lily jumped when River yowled in the other room and looked at her mother with alarm as if to ask if whatever had just happened to River was in store for her. In another minute, River emerged happily licking a lollipop that Luna had imported for purposes of happy pediatrics.

Luna waved them in. "Come in, you two. What can I do for you?"

"We're, um, actually not here for medical."

"Oh?"

"More for, ah, advice."

Luna leaned against a cabinet and put her hands in her apron pockets, smiling knowingly.

"Hmmm." Luna looked up at the ceiling. "There's a certain attractive werewolf who keeps coming to my mate for advice about *you*. I wonder if there's a coincidence."

"Advice about me? Really?" Lessie couldn't decide whether she wanted to sound surprised, hopeful, happy, or disinterested. Because, in fact, she was all of those things, except for the last. No one could accuse her of being blasé about Luna's response.

Luna grinned at the interest in Lestriv's eyes.

"Yes." She laughed. "Grey is ready to change into wolf form and stay that way until Conn stops pestering him about what to do next."

"Conn pesters the alpha about what to do next with me?" Lessie felt her face growing hot and knew that she must be blushing tomato red.

Lily noticed it. "What's wrong, Mama? Are you sick?"

"No, no, not at all," she reassured Lily while Luna reached into the jar of lollipops and withdrew a cherry distraction.

"I will tell you what I can, but I'm a paramedic. Sort of. Not a counselor."

Glancing toward Lily, Lestriv said, "We're going to need to talk in C-O-D-E."

"Sure. You first."

"I loved my mate very much." Luna's smile fell as she nodded, looking more concerned than amused. "And he's only been gone for a short time. That's why my feelings are… I don't know how you keep track of all these potions and things." She waved at the cabinets and shelves. "It's so *confusing*."

Lily's inquisitive eyes followed her mother's gesture as her attention was drawn to all the various herbs, ointments, concoctions, and remedies.

Luna glanced toward the shelves. "Perhaps it's not actually as confusing as it seems. You know that werewolves are a fun-loving bunch who live life to the fullest. When they lose someone, they pour themselves into grieving and then go on. There are no rules or judgments about how or when they go on.

"Did you know that Grey lost someone? His mate, I mean?"

Lestriv's head canted to the side. "No. I didn't."

"A long time ago." Luna smiled. "He has grandchildren." Lessie tried to imagine that. As a human, the concept was strange because Stalkson Grey seemed far too young and vigorous to be a grandfather. "It was a long time in between his loss and our meeting, but I'd like to think that if it had been a short time, the outcome would have been the same." She lifted one shoulder in a pretty shrug. "When it's right, it's right."

Lessie gave her confidante a warm smile. "You're wrong, Luna. You *are* a counselor and you've helped very much. Thank you."

"Anytime."

Lessie turned back at the doorway and whispered, "What was wrong with River?"

Luna laughed and held up a dried red bean with a pair of tweezers. "Better in the pot than in the ear I always say."

WHEN LESSIE ARRIVED back at her little cabin, Conn was waiting on the porch. She was so relieved to see him, after three days away, that she barely stopped herself from rushing forward. She'd feared that she'd left him with the impression that she had no interest in him as a helper or as a male.

"Conn." She looked happy to see him and sounded a little breathless, but Conn was afraid he was falling victim to seeing and hearing what he wanted to see and hear. "I was afraid that I'd scared you away."

His brows drew together. He looked intense,

then confused, then incredulous. "Scared me away?" After a couple of seconds he laughed out loud. "What do you imagine you might do to scare me? Much less scare me away?"

Lessie relaxed into his good humor and returned his laughter. "Silly. I know."

"Aye," he said as she stepped onto the porch and let his shadow fall over her.

"Mama and Luna were talking about you," said Lily, between licks with a cherry-red tongue.

Conn's eyes cut slowly from Lily to Lestriv as his mouth spread into a wolfish grin. "Were they now?"

"Uh-huh," said Lily as her mother glared at her.

"And what were they sayin' then?"

"What do you have to trade?" asked Lily.

Lestriv's mouth dropped open in shock. "Why you little…"

"Now, now, mama wolf," said Conn. "I'll handle this. What is it ye're wantin', Lily?"

"Bison rides. Every day for fifty years."

"One bison ride tomorrow after ye've finished yer chores," Conn countered.

"Every day for a week?" Lily asked hopefully.

"One bison ride tomorrow, no matter what,

and one the day after if yer mama says ye've been good."

Lily chanced at glance at her mother's face and concluded that her mother was not going to say she'd been "good" for a long time. "One bison ride tomorrow, no matter what, and one the day after, no matter what?"

"Done." Conn held his hand down low for Lily to slap, which she did, leaving a sticky feeling that he tried to ignore. "Now tell me everythin'."

"Wait just a minute!" Lestriv interjected.

Conn's wolfy grin resumed. "What's worryin' ye, woman? Are ye keepin' secrets that interest me, then? There's nothin' in the world I want more than to hear what the child has to say."

"Dagnabit!" said Lily. "I could have gotten more."

"Why you little…" Lessie didn't think she could have been more shocked than she had been when Lily first initiated the negotiation. Her daughter's cunning seemed to far outdistance her years in savant style.

"Shhhh," Conn said. "Let the lass speak."

"Well," Lily began dramatically by drawing out the word, "Luna said that you're always pestering the alpha."

Conn drew back, and looked a little horrified. His sudden discomfort made Lessie smile. "If you start a negotiation with a child, you can't be sure where it will lead," she said with satisfaction.

Lily continued. "Mama said her feelings are confusing." Just as quickly as it had come, Conn's discomfort was overtaken by a smug, knowing look. When his gaze pivoted toward Lessie, it was her turn to feel awkward.

"I was talking about Luna's cabinets full of medicines," Lessie offered weakly.

Lily went on, "Then Luna said the alpha is a grandpa and something about when it's right, it's right."

Lessie looked like she might be feeling a little peaked.

"Thank ye, Lily. I will give ye bison rides this one time. But I also want ye to promise that ye will never again bargain with someone else's secrets."

Lily screwed up her face. "Why?"

"Because 'tis no' right."

"Well," she said, "then why was it okay this time?"

Lestriv crossed her arms in front of her chest

and cocked her head, waiting to see how Conn was going to extricate himself from a double bind argument.

Conn didn't miss a beat. "'Twas a test to see if ye'd actually betray yer own mother." He shook his head and tsked. "And I feel terrible about the bison rides because ye should no' be rewarded for such thin's. And ye can be sure that ye ne'er will be again."

Lily's face fell into a heartbreaking crumple. "Are you mad at me?"

Lestriv's mouth fell open in shock again. She glowered at Lily. "And you're not worried about whether or not *I'm* mad at you?"

Lily looked at Lestriv without concern and said, "No. You *have* to forgive me. You're my mama."

Lessie's head fell to her chest in resignation before she looked up at Conn. "I guess that says it all."

Without taking his eyes off Lessie, Conn said, "No, Lily, I'm no' mad at ye. Would ye go inside now and wash the sticky stuff off yer fingers?"

"Okay," she said.

Once she was inside, Conn closed the door and quickly pulled Lestriv into a kiss before she had a chance to think about it. Or say no.

Her resistance gave way to the warmth of the kiss before she made a conscious decision to allow it. Her body didn't ask her brain for permission before going soft in his hands. When he pulled back, he heard her tiny moan and saw that her eyes were closed. That gave Conn encouragement enough to think he might venture teasing just a little.

"Ye'll have to help me, Lessie. I've ne'er mounted a human. Does this enraptured look on yer bonny face mean ye like my kisses?"

When she opened her eyes he thought he saw a flash of irritation. "You're the skillful lover, aren't you? I'm sure all the females crave your kisses, Conn."

When she started to pull away, he knew that he'd misjudged the timing of his playfulness. His big hands held her in place, while his voice, low and raspy, seemed to rumble in his chest. "Do no' care what the other females crave."

That pronouncement made Lessie feel curiously shy as well as flattered. She stepped back, reached up to tidy her hair, and said, "We'll see you soon then?"

His chin dipped. "Soon."

He watched as she stepped inside and closed the door before ambling toward the alpha's lodge.

"Conn. I'm glad you're here. Could you take a message to Liulf? My friend was just here."

"The demon?"

"Yes. He's taking our request for arms to Black Swan."

Conn nodded slowly. "Aye. Anything else?"

"We should have an answer in a few days. He's also going to tell Win what's happened. It may impact the rest of the tribe's decision about migrating here. Circumstances have changed greatly."

"Aye. They have. I'll be off at nightfall. Liulf will send the message on to First Colony. A few days, ye say. I expect that everythin' will change then."

Grey sat and directed his full attention to his nephew. After a moment he said, "Everything changed the day the dragon shifters came."

"True enough." Conn sighed deeply.

"What's troubling you, Konochur? More trouble with the widow Clear Eyes?"

"I wish you would no' call her that. She should not be defined by a wolf who's no longer here."

"Very well. I will call her Lestriv, if you prefer." Changing the subject, he looked toward the kitchen. "The smell of Luna's venison stew has been torturing me all afternoon. Have some with us before you go."

Conn wasn't unaffected by the heavenly aroma either. He smiled, eager to let his uncle know he regretted being abrupt. "Aye. I will. And I thank ye."

BLACK SWAN READILY agreed to supply the weapons necessary for defense. They were already invested in their alliance with two of the three werewolf tribes on Lunark and would honor that relationship without question.

Some of the members of the Elk Mountain Tribe who had stayed behind in Loti Dimension had been balking at the prospect of migrating. But when they heard about the impending war with dragon shifters, their attitudes changed quickly. Every one to the last of them stepped forward to pledge their commitment to a new world, saying no tick-carrying dragon shifters would overcome their kinsmen while they were above ground to stop it. It seemed that even werewolves who had grown as complacent as hibernating bears could be stirred to action by the suggestion of a fight worth their attention.

In a coincidence that was fortunate for the wolf residents of Lunark, those two events dovetailed each other beautifully. Just as the New Scotia wolves had transported the necessities of a new life when they immigrated, so would the tail end of the Elk Mountain tribe serve as weapons mules. The Black Swan team assigned to train the wolves on the use of modern weaponry sorted out who would carry what and every Elk Mountainer, from youngest to oldest, carried something useful if they could stand upright and walk.

The demon, Deliverance, recruited his daughter, Litha, and her friend, Kellareal to help transport two hundred odd werewolves, with arms, through the passes. Some of the larger equipment had to be disassembled and carried in pieces along with tools to reassemble, maintain, and make repairs if necessary.

The Black Swan training team consisted of a force of nine volunteer knights with heavy weapons experience. On the one hand, they were skeptical about training absolute beginners with no weapons experience. On the other hand, they were sympathetic to the plight of the werewolf colonists as it had been explained to them, mostly because of their respect and admiration for one of the knights who was a quarter werewolf, Glendennon Catch.

He also asked for temporary leave from his team so that he could join the volunteers. Since he wasn't heavy-weapons qualified, he had to take a crash course. But he was a quick study and passed his test after a forty-eight-hour session. Glen was excited by the prospect of encountering others who were human/werewolf hybrids. Even if they were all children.

THERE WERE SECTIONS of territory between the three tribes where paths were becoming visually evident because coordination required constant runners. The Council eventually voted to concede on the matter of communications as well as arms, temporarily. So the alphas and their two co-seconds were outfitted with walkie-talkie units and taught how to use them.

Ken was the first to recognize the danger posed by the paths. They were creating a map of travel habits that, when viewed from the air, might as well be an arrow saying "watch for tasty werewolves here". Liulf immediately understood the implications and used his new walkie-talkie to contact the other two alphas and suggest that those traveling between tribes choose alternate routes, avoiding the paths, and never going the exact same way twice. It would be a long time before the bare ground would regrow and cover evidence of wear, but that could work in their favor if dragons tried to watch the paths on a full moon night.

While all semblance of normalcy had been left behind once the dragon shifters made a statement of intent with a graphic example of three dead werewolves, New Elk Mountain was thrown into near chaos by almost doubling its size overnight. The new arrivals were being sheltered by residents until new housing could be built. Within a day Grey was already hearing about temper flares caused by overcrowding. He was beginning to second guess his decision to allow the immigrants to come when everything was so uncertain and when expanding the settlement would be so difficult.

Adolescents were set as watchmen so that adults could work at building without needing to also watch the skies. When Konochur showed up, Grey explained that they had needed to temporarily give his room to a family of four. With a twinkle in his eye, he suggested that Conn seek housing elsewhere. Perhaps with a young widow who was not hosting Elk Mountainers. It seemed that none of the new arrivals wanted to shelter with a human and a half werewolf.

Konochur was infuriated. "She's been openly ostracized?"

"No. No. I will not allow anyone to disrespect the humans in our tribe. The new wolves will get used to the fact that we're a mixed culture or they'll have me to deal with." His mouth twitched at the corners. "I hear that even the alpha's wife is human."

That seemed to calm Conn a bit. "Goin' to check on Lessie and Lily. If she'll no' have me for the night, save me a pallet by your hearth."

Grey smiled and put a heavy hand on Conn's shoulder. "We can use another strong back to help us get cabins up quickly. I'm glad you're here."

Conn nodded goodbye and began striding toward Lessie's house.

When he stepped onto the porch, he heard a

feminine voice a few yards away call to him. "Not there, Conn. She and the child are working the vegetable garden."

"Thank ye kindly, BlueFire."

Conn found his two girls working the neatly hoed rows, making sure that no unwanted plants claimed rainwater or crowded seedling carrots.

Lessie's first warning of Konochur's approach was a high pitched shriek.

"Conn!" Lily jumped up and ran to him. Lestriv turned to watch as Conn picked her up and spun her around laughing, holding her high, as if she weighed nothing. Lessie couldn't have suppressed a smile if she'd wanted to and thought that no mother could resist the emotional pull of hearing her child squeal with joy. Especially when the child had lost her father.

He set Lily on her feet and turned toward Lessie, still squatting in the rows pulling weeds. When she looked up, his grin resolving to a smile. "Hello Lestriv."

"Hello Konochur."

For a few moments Conn said nothing. He simply continued to look at Lessie as if he was drinking her in.

"Can I help you with the weedin'?"

"We're just done." She rose to her feet and wiped her hands on her apron. "We haven't seen you for a bit. Been busy with the weapons training?"

"Aye. I have. I hope there was no' somethin' pressin' that ye needed doin'?"

"No," she said as she gathered her tools and started toward home. She cut her eyes to the side. "We're used to having you around is all."

With a firm hand on her arm, he stopped her in her tracks and turned her to face him. "Is that yer way of sayin' ye missed me?" He could tell by the way Lessie's cheeks colored that he was on the mark. "'Tis nothin' to be embarrassed about if 'tis true. I'm no' too bashful to say that I've missed ye." He glanced at Lily who was hopping in circles around them. "Both."

She glanced up at him with a smile. "Are you staying for dinner?"

"Aye. And more."

"I don't understand."

"There's no vacancy at the alpha's house. Seems your tribe's population explosion has created an unhealthy demand for space. Grey said to seek shelter with you."

Lessie's eyes widened. "The alpha told you to

stay with me?"

"Not exactly," he said slowly. "He suggested that ye might be amenable to a guest. Under the circumstances."

"I see."

Conn didn't like the fact that Lestriv looked troubled by the conversation. "I can always go to wolf and sleep on the floor."

He noticed the tension left her face with that suggestion. "Well," she began, "I'm sure something can be worked out."

DURING DINNER, LILY entertained them both with stories she'd made up. There was one about a dragon who fell in love with a butterfly and another about snakes that could wind around a wolf and smother them to death.

Lestriv didn't know whether to be pleased with her little girl's imagination or disturbed by the unusual turn of her thought process.

While Lessie cleaned up, she listened to the pleasant sound of Conn telling Lily a bedtime story that had been written centuries before. Lily had a lot of questions. *What's a cobbler? What's a piper?* Conn's explanations made Lessie smile to herself, as did his patience with Lily. Lestriv wasn't blind to the fact that he created a warmth and a hum of life in the household that was absent when he wasn't around.

She knew what he wanted from her. He'd made that plain. She also knew she wasn't ready to allow herself an attraction so soon after losing Jimmy. That and she didn't think it would be healthy for Lily to get attached to adult males who were transient. Not that it wasn't already too late for that.

Those were the thoughts that whirled round and round inside her head as she helped Lily get ready for bed. As if Lily could read her mother's mind, she asked, "Will you still be here tomorrow, Conn?" The expression on her face was so innocently hopeful, it tore at the heartstrings of both adults.

He opened his mouth to respond, but Lessie answered. "Yes. He'll be here tomorrow."

Lessie closed the door to Lily's tiny room and made her way to the table where they'd had dinner. "How is the training going?"

"The knights seem to be pleased enough. Sometimes I think they're surprised that werewolves are clever. I can no' figure out why they'd be expectin' us to be stupid."

Lessie chuckled. "I'm sure they don't think that."

Conn sighed. "The weapons they brought us…" His expression grew serious as he locked her gaze to his. "It will work, Lessie. There's no question in my mind. It will work."

"I hope so, Conn. We all hope so. I don't want Lily to grow up always looking overhead in fear, not being able to venture more than a few feet away from a structure with a roof. Although," Lessie looked toward Lily's closed door then leaned in, lowering her voice to a whisper, "I'm not sure roofs would protect us if the dragons made up their minds on utter destruction."

That was punctuated with a shiver that raised Conn's protective instincts, but also made him painfully hard. He attempted to surreptitiously adjust himself in the chair. He didn't want to find out what Lestriv would think of the blooming big erection he'd sprouted just from watching one little shiver travel up her spine.

He swallowed to find voice because his mouth had gone dry. "'Twill all be over soon. We're goin' to rid this beautiful place of buggerin' flyin' reptiles. When 'tis done, we'll be pickin' up little bits of dragon shifter for a long time to come." Conn's reassurance dropped to a soothing tone. Lestriv's reaction began with a nod and ended with a yawn. "Too much diggin' in the garden. Would ye like me to heat enough water for a bath?"

"That sounds like heaven, but," she laughed softly, "I don't think I could stay awake long enough. I'm keeping the offer though. Maybe I'll ask tomorrow or…"

"When'er you wish."

"So…" she began shyly, "you said you wouldn't mind sleeping on the floor? As wolf?"

He was disappointed not to be invited into the warm bed with the curves that were only made more delectable by the swell of her belly, but hadn't expected it.

He nodded as he walked toward the hearth. "I'll just sit here in the chair and tend the fire until I'm ready."

Lestriv's cabin consisted of a main room and a small anteroom just big enough for Lily and her single cot. The double bed sat against the wall opposite the fireplace so that Lessie could see everything in the room when she was turned toward the hearth. She'd changed into a long linen nightgown in Lily's room, said goodnight to Konochur, crawled into bed, and was asleep almost immediately.

Although there was nothing to fear in New Elk Mountain, at least there hadn't been before the dragon shifters arrived, she recognized that she felt more relaxed and secure when Conn was there. That constant tension and unease of single parenthood abated as if on some level she felt the responsibility to keep Lily safe was shared.

Sometime later she heard a rustle and roused from her sleep. When she opened her eyes, Conn was removing his clothes. She watched in fascination as he stripped down to skin. Like many of the New Elk Mountain males, he'd taken to wearing buttery soft doeskin pants. When he turned to lay them over the chair, he glanced at Lessie and saw that she was awake and staring at his nakedness.

Konochur, like other werewolves, couldn't really grasp the human concept of modesty, but he knew he had even less reason to be modest than most. With that thought he turned so that Lestriv could look her fill and see what he had to offer, as a male. Not a handyman or caretaker. As a lover.

Lessie thought the right thing to do was to look away, but she couldn't find the will. When he'd made eye contact with her and realized she was watching, she'd thought she'd seen his eyes fire with heat, but it was probably her imagination or the momentary reflection of firelight when he turned.

She had no doubt that Konochur was the most desirable male on Lunark or anywhere so far as she knew. The combination of his beauty, confidence, and sexy smiles had her constantly wondering why he wanted her. After a couple of minutes, he grinned at Lessie then changed into a wolf so quickly it took her breath away.

Konochur was as beautiful as a wolf as he was as a man. The fur along his head and back was the same blue-black color as his hair in human form, while his chest and belly were silver. He stalked toward Lessie and, when he reached the bed, bumped her with his nose.

"What?" she asked. When he did it again, she couldn't suppress a smile and moved over.

Conn placed his front paws on the bed and boosted the rest of his body up with a little rear end hop. He collapsed with a masculine huff, lay his head near hers and gave up a mighty sigh of contentment. Lessie's fingers itched to reach out and touch the fur that was just inches from her hand. After a while her resistance gave way to her overriding desire to know what it felt like. She ran her hand along his back. The top layer of fur was a little coarse, but there was another layer just underneath, that was silky to the touch.

Konochur turned his head so that he could give her wrist a little lick of approval with a warm tongue. She grinned in the dim light and said, "Thank you."

CHAPTER 7

✖

THE BATTLE PLAN was simple. Plan A. Take the top of the mountain off, hopefully killing all the dragon shifters at once, in the nest. Plan B. If some of them survived, chase them through the air with camera-fitted drones. Plan C. If any survived Plan A *and* Plan B, assume they would take to the air. That meant wait for them to show themselves, then shoot point-blank rapid-fire rocket blasters at them until nothing remains.

It hadn't taken the volunteer knights long to identify which werewolves had the most aptitude for technological warfare. A few simple tests rendered more than enough candidates for drone controller. The werewolves were not only highly intelligent, but had much quicker reaction times than humans.

Likewise, it wasn't hard to separate candidates for hunting with rocket blasters. As Glendennon Catch put it, "You pick the biggest sons-of-bitches available and hope they can aim in the general direction of the target." Liulf was put into that group. He didn't know whether to be proud of being big and strong or insulted that the knights referred to the blaster unit as The Meatheads.

Meteorological equipment wasn't one of the technologies they imported from Loti. So they had to rely on methods of weather prediction that were older, but just as reliable. They needed a day so perfectly clear that hiding in clouds wouldn't be an option for dragons in flight.

The knights, who had signed on for training, decided unanimously that they would stay long enough to be sure the Lunark werewolves were rid of dragon shifters. Command Central had been set up in the dense forest of the valley beneath the mountain the dragons had defaced. In some ways the tall trees were better protection than buildings.

All the wolves who had roles to play had said goodbye to their families at dusk the night before and traveled during the night to reach the gathering point. A few had come with a clothing pack tied or strapped to their wolf form, but most hadn't bothered. At first the bodies of naked werewolves, male and female, threw the Black Swan knights off balance, but even they were surprised by how fast they adjusted.

Conn had made light of his part because he didn't want to upset Lestriv or have her needlessly worry, but truthfully, he'd been assigned one of the most dangerous jobs. He was part of the crew that would climb the mountain to assess the success or failure of Plan A.

Most of the dragons were killed by the first drone strike. Had they been in dragon form, some might have survived with injuries, but they made a habit of spending their nights drinking themselves into a stupor and sleeping wherever they passed out, in infinitely more fragile, human form. Between the fact that they had built themselves a mountaintop fortress and the fact that they were unquestionably the top of the food chain on Lunark, they believed themselves invulnerable to attack.

They had deliberately sought out a world without technology-driven weaponry and had further insured the safety of their nest by showing the locals how easy it was for dragons to extinguish their insignificant lives. The inhabitants of Lunark didn't even present enough of a danger to post a lookout.

Grenhelde had been in the top of the highest tower nursing hurt feelings and a skin of blood wine. She'd been rejected by Tharenvolf for the fourth time in three centuries and each time was worse than the time before. That night the rejection had been punctuated with a backhand that sent her stumbling into a table of food. Her humiliation was made complete by a response of raucous laughter from the witnesses. She would have sought adoption by another nest if it wasn't for the fact that her brother and two cousins, her only remaining family, were part of that nest. After seeing them join in laughing at her humiliation, she was reevaluating the value of those relationships. Alone with drink to help dull the pain.

The first explosion separated the top of the tower from the rest of the structure. Since the lower part of the fortress had been targeted, it was more or less pulverized, but oddly, the section of tower, where Grenhelde had been drinking alone, remained intact. It tumbled down the opposite side of the mountain, crumbling along the way. As soon as enough of the stones had broken away, she shifted to her dragon form which was capable of taking a lot of abuse. She was able to break up the rest of the stones in transformation and fly free of the tumbling ruin, but not without injury. Before shifting she'd sustained cuts, slashes, bruises, and a sprained elbow, which hurt enough to make her whimper with each beat of her wings.

Grenhelde's brother had been one of those killed in the first bomb volley. There were four dragons, other than Grenhelde that survived only because they had passed out on the rock "courtyard" outside the fortress, mostly because of drunkenness, but partly because the cool night air made their reptile cores sluggish. The explosions woke them up quickly, but not fast enough to flee unscathed. Each one of the four had taken shrapnel wounds of various degrees of severity.

When Grenhelde reached the site that had been their new home, she had planned to fly high enough to get an overview of the situation, but the sounds of pops and whistles made her change course and land behind the rubble that had been a fortress. Peeking over the rocks she watched as each of the four dragons bore down on the location from which the werewolves were launching the modern equivalent of grenade rockets.

The dragons roared furious protests, but each in turn met humility when he was blasted and plummeted from the sky. Pop. Whistle. Thud. Pop. Whistle. Thud.

From her secret perch, Grenhelde continued to watch the werewolves confirm the dragon shifter deaths with keen eyes that could focus from a great distance. When some of the werewolves began to climb the mountain, with apparent intent to make sure there were no survivors, she turned and flew to the far side of a great rock that rose from the sandy expanse on the back side of the mountain range. And there she began to nurse her wounds and contemplate what it meant to be the last. The last dragon.

CHAPTER 8

✕

AFTER A THREE-NIGHT-LONG joint celebration of the werewolves' victory, the Black Swan knights said their goodbyes and left. The Council members agreed that they would divide the weapons among them, seal them against damage from the elements, and bury them in places only known to the alphas and their seconds.

Lunark quickly returned to normal. Children ran and played outside in the sun, while adults soaked in the joyful sounds. Likewise, sheep and bison could graze during the daytime and hunters could hunt wherever, whenever there was need.

The New Elk Mountain tribe turned their attention to building to accommodate the expansion that reunited the tribe and made them whole again.

Konochur continued to court Lestriv according to the model of patience his uncle insisted would bear fruit. Eventually.

Enjoying the sight of Lily running free in the fields, he had turned to Lessie with the sexy grin she had come to look forward to. She allowed the corners of her mouth to twitch because she knew that what would come out of his mouth next would be something completely inappropriate and blush-worthy, but just as sexy as his grin.

While the two adults were busy flirting, Lily was chasing a fuchsia colored butterfly from one wild flower to another. Conn searched Lessie's face for confirmation that her feelings matched his, when he saw her eyes shift to something behind him. In less than a second her face froze into a mask of fright and she shrieked Lily's name.

All werewolves were quick, but Konochur was quicker than most. Just before he changed into his werewolf form, he screamed for Lily to lie down flat. She turned toward him and looked stunned, but thankfully, for once, did as he said without question. He knew that the dragon would have a harder time grabbing her if she was prone flat on the ground.

As Conn sprinted toward Lily he was trying to estimate his chances of reaching her before the dragon did and didn't like the result of his calculations. As he pushed with all his might, he begged his body to give him more, to stretch his limbs further, stretch his nostrils wider, make his muscles crave speed and eat up the distance that separated him from Lestriv's child.

DURING THE TWO weeks since the attack, Grenhelde had not shifted back to two-legged form. That had enabled her body to heal faster, but her brain as a dragon wasn't nearly as adept at complex thinking. The dragon brain fixated on the fact that werewolves had destroyed her home and killed everyone in her nest. Except her. Though she had been ready to leave them before the attack, she was sore with the indignation and insult of massacre.

As she descended into something akin to depression, her only hope was that she could visit some of her misery on the creatures who had caused her suffering. Every day she climbed to the ruins of the fortress and looked over. Even in the darkness of her madness, she knew that, if she bided her time, there would be an opportunity to give the wolves a taste of cold vengeance.

Her elbow had gotten strong enough so that she could shift and fly without too much pain. The pains that remained weren't of the body, but the mind.

CONN'S CLOTHES SHREDDED around him as he ran with ears laid back against his head signaling that he would burst his own heart to protect the little girl he loved like his own child.

The dragon saw him rushing toward her prey, but didn't worry. She could easily swat him away with her mighty tail. She could tell by the intensity of his speed, that the prey meant something to him. And she was glad. That moment of elation caused her to flap her wings again, gauging the downdraft so that she could coast on the breeze, talons at the ready, to snatch the tiny thing and carry her away screaming while the wolf pack wailed and regretted the day they had thought to challenge dragons.

Lessie had begun screaming for help as soon as Conn started running for Lily. Several of the New Elk Mountain wolves were close enough to respond, including Stalkson Grey. All those who were close enough to see watched in horror as the dragon dipped to grab Lily. But just as Conn had guessed, it was harder for the dragon to grab her from the ground.

Grenhelde hesitated for just the extra second that Konochur needed to reach Lily. When the dragon came close to the ground, he sprang into the air with a mighty leap born of desperation and locked his powerful jaws onto her throat. With werewolf ears, Conn heard Lily's little girl sobs and it tore at his heart. He knew that her mother would reach her and comfort her and that gave him the peace he needed to keep his attention single-mindedly focused on the purpose at hand.

To not let go.

To never let go.

Three of the wolves had shifted while running and were now trying to follow the path of the dragon's flight from the ground. Normally, that would have been hopeless, but Grenhelde was quickly weakening from the loss of blood pouring from her neck and running down her body. She left a trail of falling red liquid in the air.

Conn tried not to swallow the dragon blood, but it was impossible. It trickled down his throat and ate at his insides all the way to his stomach, burning like acid. The smell stung his eyes so badly that he was nearly blinded. He never questioned that he was going to die. He knew it. But he was determined that the dragon would die with him.

All he had to do was hang on.

At one point he thought to himself what an odd sensation it was to be hanging from his teeth high above the earth, all four paws dangling in the air.

The dragon flew closer and closer to the earth as she gradually lost both blood and the will to live. Eventually she was forced to land, dragging in ragged breaths through the wound caused by the werewolf's teeth.

Still, Konochur held onto her throat.

She fell to her side and collapsed into human form.

Still, Konochur held onto her throat.

By the time the werewolves who had been following reached them, Grenhelde was dead, but still, Konochur held onto her throat.

Stalkson Grey took human form and tried to pry Conn's jaws away from the corpse, but Conn growled a warning that couldn't be ignored and refused to let go. Grey sent the other two wolves back to the settlement with a message to have Luna prepare a sedative for Conn. One was to bring the potion as fast as possible. The other was to prepare a bison cart with a mattress and bring it to take him home.

While he waited, Grey talked to Conn in soothing tones, assuring him that the dragon was dead, that Lestriv and Lily were both safe, but whenever he moved toward Conn's jaws, he got a growl and raised hackles for his trouble.

"Not ready to give up yet? Very well. We can wait a bit longer then."

Half an hour later a wolf came charging toward them with a jar tied around his neck. Grey took the jar and waited for the wolf to shift.

"She says to open the lid and hold it under his nose until he goes to sleep."

Grey lost no time in doing exactly that.

Conn growled, but was caught in a dilemma. He would have to let go of the dragon shifter's neck to stop Grey from putting him to sleep. And he wasn't going to do that. So he growled and threatened as best he could while refusing to let go of the dragon. He snarled his protest and shook the female back and forth, which snapped the neck of Grenhelde's lifeless body. Without enough energy left to remain standing, he fell over, his big chest heaving from exhaustion and strain.

After another minute of holding Luna's jar under Conn's nose his growls became softer and his eyelids were barely staying open. In another minute after that, he was out completely, jaws gone slack.

Grey and the two other wolves hoisted Konochur's sleeping weight onto the pallet in the back of the wagon.

The alpha shifted and trotted along behind the wagon so that he could watch his nephew all the way home. Luna was standing outside her clinic waiting with a very worried-looking Lestriv by her side. As soon as Grey shifted, he turned to the cart driver.

"Send people out there to burn the body. No ceremony," he ordered.

The cart driver nodded and hurried away.

IN FACT, GRENHELDE had not been the last dragon. But she had been the last dragon on Lunark. The Black Swan Department of Endangered Species had been alerted that there could be a problem if the dragon shifters were not contained someplace where they would be prevented from causing harm to humans and other shifters. Perhaps they would find a solution before the next critical incident. Perhaps not.

CONN WAS UNHARMED except for the fact that he'd swallowed so much of the dragon blood and the fact that dragon blood was poisonous and highly damaging to internal organs.

Luna looked up at Lessie. "There's really nothing else to be done. The poison has to work its way through his system and he needs to heal internally. I'd say it's a blessing that he's sleeping because being awake would be painful."

"Well, he shouldn't stay here." Lessie looked around at the clinic as if it was completely unsuitable.

"Where do you think he should stay?" Luna asked softly.

Lestriv didn't hesitate. Konochur was a male who had performed a feat so heroic it would be legendary for generations of werewolves to come. She was sure there would come a time in the distant future when descendants would say it was a myth, that no werewolf could bring down a dragon alone. But Conn had done exactly that to save the life of Lessie's little girl, at great, almost surely fatal, risk to himself.

Then there was also the fact that she loved him.

"He can stay at my cottage. You can treat him there. Whatever you say he needs, that's what will be done."

Luna simply nodded. "Of course, Lestriv. That's a fine solution and one that will certainly please Konochur when he wakes."

Lessie's attention jerked to Luna. "So you're sure he will wake."

Luna bit her bottom lip and hesitated. "I wish I could promise, but the best I can do is to say that I have firsthand experience that when Conn wants something, he lets nothing stand in his way. And I'm certain he wants to live."

CHAPTER 9

✖

WHEN CONN'S EYES flew open, he tried to sort through the haze. Where was he and how did he get there? He began to see flashes of a dragon in flight, heading for Lily. He felt adrenaline prick at the nerve endings in his body as he relived a smidgeon of the terror he'd felt.

Just as the monster banked its wings and dipped toward Lily, it had lifted its head and looked at Conn. He could have sworn he saw a cruel smile distort its face. That was followed by the memory of being carried away in the air, the odd sensation of hanging by his teeth, and his determination to keep his jaws locked even if the creature flew him to dragon hell.

He remembered hearing the sounds of death throes coming from the very throat he held in the vice grip of his jaws and the sensation of descending too fast. Falling.

Jerking his gaze to the left he recognized Lessie's cabin. The fire had died down to hot glowing coals and he was glad of that because he suddenly felt too hot and needed to throw the covers back. He turned his head to the right and was stunned by the sight of Lestriv, her hair looking like a whirl of multicolored ribbons of auburn, chestnut, and amber.

There was only one thing in the world he wanted more than to reach out and touch her and that was to see Lily. He knew she must be fine, but that terror he had felt wouldn't be appeased until he saw that for himself.

He eased himself out of bed, careful not to wake Lestriv and padded quietly to Lily's little room. Willing the door not to creak, he opened it slowly, and smiled to himself when he saw her curled on her side hugging three stuffed, fur covered animals to her chest.

Closing the door, he realized there was one other thing he wanted more than to be in bed with Lessie and that was a good long piss. He almost groaned with the sweet relief of draining his bladder. Before going back to bed, he drank water like he'd had none for days. It overflowed his mouth and ran down his chest. That also felt good against his heated skin.

As he walked toward the bed, his erection sprang to full bloom in anticipation of claiming the woman who had been dallying long enough. As he was hanging in the air, jaws latched tight on the throat of a devil in dragon form, believing that he was flying toward his death, he remembered thinking that he had one and only one regret. That he'd never had the pleasure of sinking balls deep into the woman who'd been chosen for him by the whims of fate.

As his knee depressed the mattress he threw the covers to the foot of the bed and slowly began pushing Lestriv's long nightgown up her body.

She opened her eyes in surprise, then realizing what was happening, opened her eyes wider.

"Conn, you…"

Whatever she was going to say next was smothered by his kiss, and her gasp that took his breath into her body. His hand stopped at the juncture of her thighs to administer some much needed, expert attention. When the delicious sensation made her cry out without warning, her hand flew to her mouth to muffle the sound so that she wouldn't wake Lily.

Lessie's look of disbelief changed to a look of

concern without warning. Her hands grabbed for his face. "Conn. You're still feverish. We can't…"

"Aye, we can. And we will."

"But you're still sick."

"I'm well enough."

Conn's eyes were sparkling with lust and mischief. The look of his skin, flushed with fever, begged to be touched. After pulling the night-gown over Lessie's head, he stared at her body as if he'd never seen a woman unclothed. She fought the impulse to cover herself and had an internal debate about arguing the point of his fever further, but instead she said, "You weren't really assigned to help me. Were you?"

His gaze jerked to her eyes as if he was looking for something. Seeming satisfied with what he saw, he grinned and shook his head no. Then he plumped one breast and ran his tongue around her nipple without taking his eyes from her face. After bringing the other nipple to a peak hard as a pebble, he began worshipping her body with kisses, strokes, and tiny nibbles that caused her to arch away from the straw mattress.

Whenever she tried to urge him to hurry, he just looked at her, grinned, shook his head no, then proceeded to make love to her with a masterfully slow and painstaking deliberation. By the time she felt his cock probe her entrance she was covered in a slick sheen of perspiration that matched his. It caused what Lessie would always remember as the most erotic sound of their bodies slapping together rhythmically.

Like most women who work with their hands, she kept her nails short, but not so short that Conn didn't revel in the pleasure pain of feeling them digging into his back. When she peaked, her teeth latched onto his neck and bit down in a delicious crescendo of ravishment while the werewolf jerked once, growled deep in his chest, and trembled as his seed spilled inside her.

Lessie felt an inexplicable tear race down her cheek and reached to wipe it away before Conn saw it and misunderstood. It wasn't a sad tear or a happy tear. It was simply more emotion than her body could contain. She had released much more than an orgasm. She'd let go of her first love and given herself to another, body and soul.

Konochur collapsed beside her, careful not to put his weight on the swell of her abdomen. Turning his head on the pillow he treated Lessie to such a captivating, and very wolfy, smile of male satisfaction that it made her heart flutter.

"Will you be leaving us now?" She blurted it out before she could stop herself.

Conn's smile turned to a look of confusion. "Leavin' ye? I do no' understand ye."

She looked away. "I mean, you know…"

He raised himself on an elbow so that he could look down at her. With brows drawn together, he said, "No. I do no' know."

"I mean, are you done with me since I've let you in my bed?"

He continued to stare as if he was uncomprehending right up until he threw himself to his back and nearly howled with laughter.

Lessie sat up, scowling. "What's so funny?"

When he got himself under control, he said simply, "Humans."

"Humans?"

"Aye. Humans. Did ye think that I've spent all this time givin' flyin' lessons to chickens, and carryin' baskets of potatoes, and mendin' livestock fences… No' to mention provin' that I'm willin' to give my life for my family. Ye think I'd do these thin's for a fuck?" Lessie's mouth dropped open. "In case ye're tryin' to think up an answer, that question was rhetorical. That means…"

She narrowed her eyes. "I know what it means."

"The answer is no. I did no'. I'm no' a farmer, Lessie. I'm a warrior. For hundreds of years my brothers and I kept a country resplendent with desirable coastline, easily accessed by maraudin' barbarians intact. But here I am throwin' chickens and carryin' corn... I think I've shown ye that there's nothin' I would no' do to have ye accept me as yer mate. And nothin' I would no' do to keep my family safe."

Her eyes glazed with mist when he said 'family'. She took his meaning very well. He was promising to be her husband, but he was also promising to be father to her children. All she could manage to say was, "Mate?"

His face and voice softened as he settled himself over her, "Do no' behave as if this comes as a surprise to ye."

"Well..."

"That is no' the way to begin that sentence." He rocked his body into her, which was distracting to say the least.

"You cannot possibly be, uh, ready again this soon."

"Reach down and take hold of the livin' proof. I've been wantin' this for a long time." She shifted and squirmed a little, which made proof more than evident without the use of hands. "So?" Conn's voice dropped to a sexy rumble as he sucked her earlobe into his mouth. "Are ye havin' me to mate then?"

He pulled back so as to better see her face. When her radiant smile appeared he let out the breath he'd been holding and the tiny lines around his eyes smoothed away.

"I'm havin' ye then."

"When did ye figure out that the Council did no' assign me to look after ye?"

"When I noticed that the other two widows didn't have a gorgeous unmated werewolf regularly calling."

Conn laid his head back on the pillow for a moment. "Ye think I'm gorgeous?"

And she laughed.

WHILE LESTRIV KNEW that there was a place in her heart that would always belong to Jimmy Clear Eyes, she also knew that Conn was right. Jimmy would want their children to have a strong protector who loved and cherished them. And he would want Lessie to be happy.

EPILOGUE

✕

LUNA AND HER apprentices had shooed Conn outside when Lessie's labor began in earnest. And there he had waited in the darkness for hours. Hearing her in such distress was the hardest thing he'd ever done. He walked in circles. A couple of times he'd peeked inside only to have three women yell at him to, "Get out."

Finally, he decided to change into wolf form for comfort. At least he'd be warm. He lay down in the middle of the passage between buildings that would have been considered a road in Scotia and put his head on his paws. On hearing Lessie's screams intensify, he rose, turned around, and flopped down with agitation. When she screamed again he lifted his head, which happened to be facing east. As the first sunbeam pierced the blackness of night he heard a baby's cry.

He changed to human form and burst into the room.

With sweat trickling down the side of her face, Luna looked at him and smiled. "It's a boy, Conn."

"A boy." He whispered it with so much awe that he made it sound like no other male baby had ever been born. "Lessie?"

"She's fine. Just sleeping. She deserves it. She worked really hard."

Luna's two midwife apprentices finished knotting the umbilical cord, wiped the baby off with warm water, wrapped him in a cotton cloth, and handed him to Luna.

She in turn said, "Here's your son, Conn. Take him." Conn looked at Luna with a horrified expression and shook his head vigorously. She laughed. "Don't worry. Look. Put your hand under his head to support his neck and let him rest in the crook of your arm, just like that."

Feeling the pliant warmth next to his body made Conn feel strange. He swallowed the lump in his throat.

"He's beautiful," Luna said. "Perfect in every way."

"Perfect," Conn repeated as he swayed back

and forth with the baby in his arm.

WHEN LESTRIV WOKE, the first thing she saw was Konochur's smile. The second thing she saw was the bundle in his arms. She reached for the baby. As Conn gingerly placed him in his mother's arms, he said, "We have a son, Lessie. Perfect in every way. And I know his name."

Lestriv managed a small smile. She had been part of a werewolf tribe long enough to know that werewolves approached naming like it was a mystic ritual. It could be said that they were superstitious about it, but oddly, they seemed to always get it right.

"What will you call him?" she asked as she placed a kiss on the tiny forehead.

"Mac ar Maidin."

She repeated it twice. "What does it mean?"

"Son of the Mornin'."

ALSO BY VICTORIA DANANN

You can help me stay in business by taking a minute to leave reviews on the books you've read. New readers are more likely to discover my books when there are more reviews.

Victoria Danann

SUBSCRIBE TO MY MAIL LIST for exclusive interviews and News First Announcements!

http://eepurl.com/bN4fHX

Website

victoriadanann.com

Facebook Author Page

facebook.com/victoriadanannbooks

Victoria's Facebook Fan Group

facebook.com/groups/772083312865721

Twitter

twitter.com/vdanann

Pinterest

pinterest.com/vdanann

BEST PARANORMAL ROMANCE SERIES

Three Years In A Row! –

Knights of Black Swan

BEST PARANORMAL ROMANCE NOVEL (GENERAL) –

A Summoner's Tale

BEST PARNORMAL ROMANCE NOVEL (Vampires & Shifters) –

Moonlight

BEST PARANORMAL ROMANCE NOVEL (Vampires) –

Solomon's Sieve

Made in the USA
San Bernardino, CA
31 May 2016